Oskar's Quest

Klippor
PRESS

> *'With much love to my son, Sammy,*
> *who as a young boy inspired me*
> *to tell him this story at bedtime.'*

Published by *Klippor* Press.

Paperback Release: 2019.

Cover design and Illustrations by Gabrielle Vickery.
Book Layout by David Cronin.

Flap-flap! Flap-flap!

The wings of the blue bird flapped one last time as he landed on a flower.

"Where am I?"
Oskar muttered to himself.
Around him purple trees
groaned in the wind.
Orange grasses waved back
		and forth, as
green spiders scampered
across the white rocks.

"On Roda," a small voice answered. Oskar spun round, peering into the gloom.

Above him towered yellow and green spotted flowers, stretching as if to reach the sky.

Below him red bell-flowers looked lonely.

Oskar hopped down and perched on a flower. He glanced at the edges of the leaves, which were drooping with sadness.

"You're on the island of Roda and ouch, you are hurting me," whispered Bella, the red bell-flower.

"I'm sorry," said Oskar as he fluttered down onto the orange grass and looked up at her. The flower nodded sadly as one more leaf drifted to the ground. A drop of water followed.

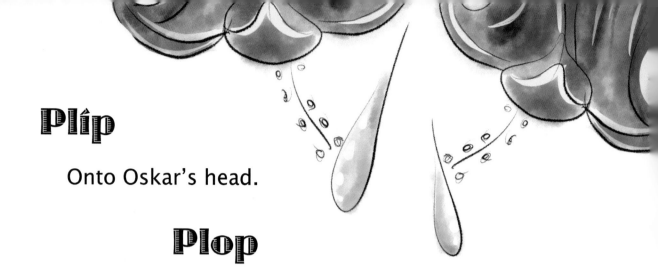

Plíp

Onto Oskar's head.

Plop

Into his eyes. Blinking Oskar saw
tiny tears roll from the inside of the red bells.

Plíp

Down along the petals.

Plop

Onto his wings. Bella was crying and
she couldn't stop.

Oskar hopped away and shook the tears from his wings.
Carefully he approached Bella who started to speak.

"Our happy songbird, Maya, has been taken by Drang,
the darkest cloud in the sky."

"It was a very stormy night and Maya sheltered right here, under my leaves.

"Drang raced along, picking up anything he could find. I tried to hold on to her. I did. I tried so hard.

"Now she is gone!

"The island is so sad . . . the music has stopped."

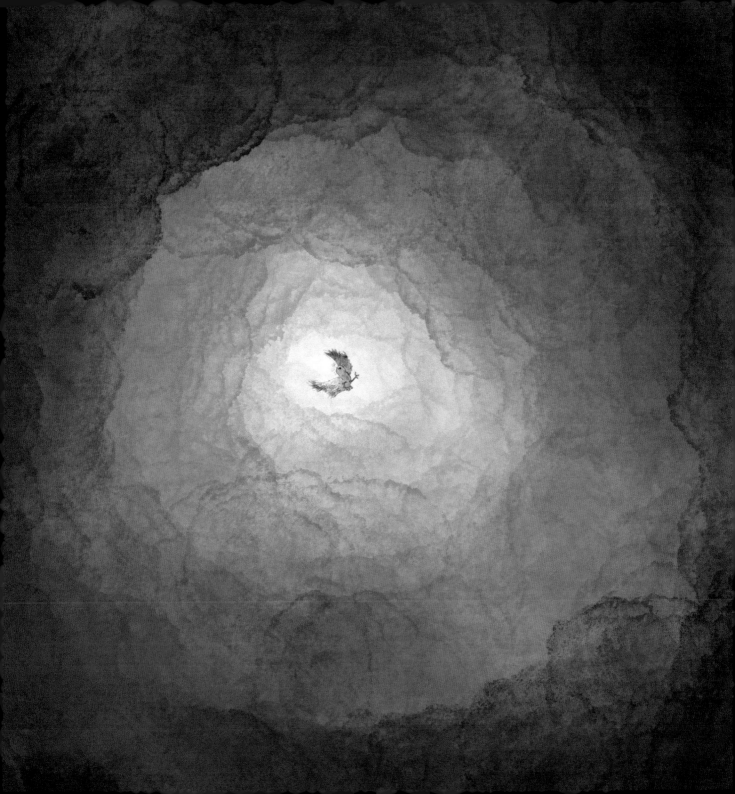

Once more Bella burst into tears.

Plíp-plop!

Plíp-plop!

Splosh

"Where is Drang? I will go and talk to him," said Oskar, much to his own surprise. He was not a brave bird. When his friends went flying on exciting adventures, Oskar stayed at home, safe in his nest.

On their latest dragon
hunting trip Oskar had
joined in but got scared.
He had turned to fly home but
lost his way in the storm
and landed on Roda. His
friends had flown away,
calling out,

"Scaredy-bird, scaredy-bird."

Their taunts echoed in his mind.

"This will not do," he murmured to himself.

"Where is Drang?" Oskar repeated, louder this time.

Bella tilted her bell upwards . . . Oskar gazed towards the sky.

There was Drang. It was the most fearsome of clouds,
the largest in the sky. Lightning flashed from its edges
and in the distance Oskar heard the crash of thunder.

"Be careful," whispered Bella.

Oskar flew away, heading in small circles up into the sky.

BOOM!

His wings tingled with fear.

Flaaash!

Oskar quivered mid-air, his feathers fluttering madly.

"I'm NOT a scaredy-bird," he told himself. He flew on.

The closer he got to the cloud, the windier it became.

Whoosh!

The strong gale sent him tumbling downwards.
Flapping wildly he recovered.

Flaaash!

Lightning struck close by.

Whoosh!

A sudden gust swept Oskar into
Drang and he landed
on the soft surface with
a bounce or two.

All was still. All was quiet. There was no storm, no thunder or lightning. "I made it," yelled Oskar into the silence. Around him swirled a bubble of misty purple fog.

"*Eeek...*"

The prolonged SPOOKY screech came from ahead.

"*Eeek...*"

As if on a trampoline Oskar hopped towards the desperate cry.

In a dazzling cage was a golden bird. It must be Maya!

She pecked at the coloured jewels on the bars of the cage. On the plush ruby red carpet lay star-shaped bowls of nuts and seeds. In a moon-shaped dish water swished gently against the sides.

In the middle of the cage stood a small tree in a pot. Maya flapped once and landed on a branch. Oskar flew on top of the cage and looked at the saddest happy songbird he had ever seen.

"*Eeek...*"

"Stop it! Please!" shouted Oskar. "Maya, I am here to save you."
Maya opened her golden beak but stopped,
swallowed her screech and hiccupped loudly. Her body
trembled with fear and hope.

"Take me home to my friends," cried Maya. "PLEASE..."

Flaaash!

Lightning struck inside the cloud revealing a large empty dome.

"I want to be your friend,"

boomed a voice.

The whole cloud shuddered.

Petrified, Oskar and Maya cowered. Suddenly Oskar flew fearlessly into the air and sang as loudly as he could.

"We want to be your friends too, but you are scaring us. Please don't shout."

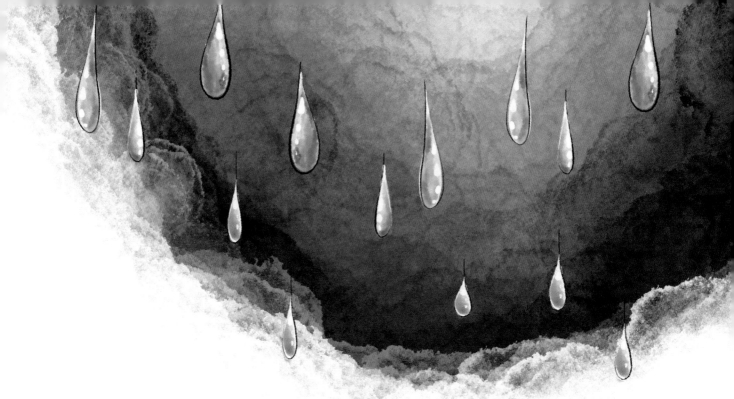

"I am so lonely," continued Drang, his booming voice slightly quieter. "On Roda I saw how happy you all were."

"Maya, I thought if you came with me you could make me happy too.

Now you are so sad, I can't stop crying."

At these words Drang heaved a giant sob and rain poured onto the island below. Inside Drang water also fell. Soon the floods drenched Oskar and Maya.

Drang is crying, Oskar realised. So that is rain — *tears from the unhappy clouds.*

"Drang, I have an idea," Oskar piped up. "Why don't you come to Roda and listen to the songs? Chat with us! You're very welcome — just don't make it too wet or windy."

Maya nodded eagerly.

Claaang!

The cage door opened and Maya flew up to Oskar,
singing with joy and thanks. Drang tried to join them with
his loud "BOOM! BOOM!"

Soon the cloud stopped and they all looked at
Roda below.

Drang lost his fierce blackness, and all the flashes and
thunder disappeared.

Together the two birds flew out of the cloud down to the island.

"Thank you for bringing us back," Maya called up to Drang. "I promise you happiness forever."

At her words all the birds, flowers and trees of Roda sang a song of celebration. The music made Drang so happy he could not help but shed a few tears of joy.

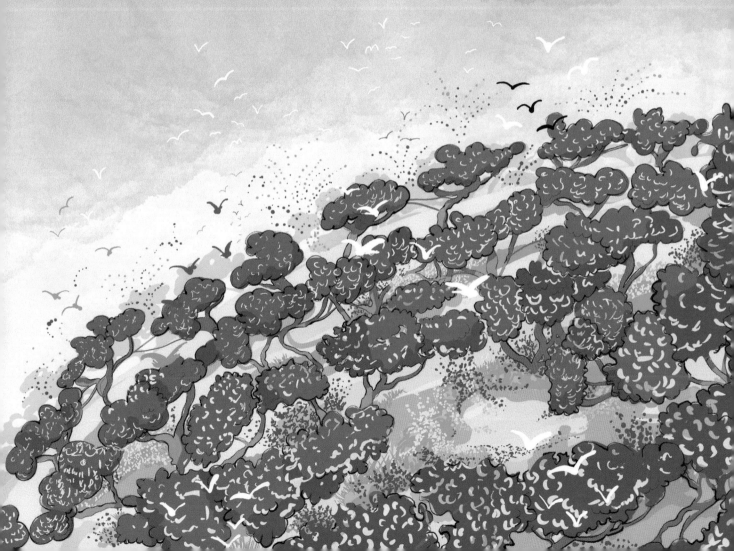

Plip-plop!

Plip-plop!

Splosh!

"Oh no," moaned Oskar. "Not again."

The extraordinary party lasted all day and at
sunset Oskar turned to Maya and Bella.

"Now I have to return home to my nest,
to my family and friends."
He flew up into the sky,
bidding farewell.

"Wait for me!" called Drang.
"I will show you the way."

Soon they met Oskar's friends, returning from their dragon hunting trip.

"Scaredy-bird! Scaredy-bird! Where have you been hiding?"

BOOM!

Flaaash!

Drang's voice thundered across the sky.

"This is Oskar – the bravest bird in the world,"
 roared Drang.

The birds shook in fright, their feathers quivering.

"Don't be scared!" Oskar called out to them.

"Come and meet my new friend, Drang. I met him on my
 adventures!"

The End

Printed in Great Britain
by Amazon